Bilal

Bridget

Betsy

Bertie

Bernie

Bonnie

Basil

Barney

Bobbie

Bia

For Rex – G.A.

For my lovely friend, Nia Roberts,
thank you for everything xx – L.P.

First published 2023 by Nosy Crow Ltd
Wheat Wharf, 27a Shad Thames, London, SE1 2XZ, UK

Nosy Crow Eireann Ltd
44 Orchard Grove, Kenmare, Co Kerry, V93 FY22, Ireland

www.nosycrow.com

ISBN 978 1 83994 327 0 (HB)
ISBN 978 1 83994 328 7 (PB)

Text by Lou Peacock
Text © Nosy Crow 2023
Illustrations © Ged Adamson 2023

A CIP catalogue record for this book is available from the British Library.

Printed in Spain

Papers used by Nosy Crow are made from wood grown in sustainable forests.

1 3 5 7 9 8 6 4 2 (HB)
1 3 5 7 9 8 6 4 2 (PB)

THE BEAR THE BOOK AND THE BLANKET

Lou Peacock

 nosy crow

Ged Adamson

Bunnies, it's Baby's bedtime.
Let's all be nice and quiet.

SHHHHHHh.

Baby is **wide awake.** Hmmm . . .

OF COURSE!

Baby needs Bear, Book and Blanket.

Bunnies, I'm going to need your help.
Yes, that's right. Let's look for Bear first.

Thank you, Bunnies.
That is a **lot** of bears!

But, oh dear, none of those
bears are Baby's bear.

Unless . . .

Bobbie . . .
have you got Baby's bear?

BOBBIE!

Give it back to Baby, please.

Thank you, Bunnies.
And thank you, Bobbie.

Look how Baby **loves** Bear!
Bear is the best bear in **all the world.**

What a happy baby!

But . . . Baby can't get to sleep
without Book and Blanket too.
Bunnies, can you help?

That's it! Off you go.

Yes, you're right. Baby's book **must**
be here somewhere, but . . . Bunnies . . .

you don't need to take **all**
the books off **all** the shelves . . .

Never mind – at least we've found it!
Yes, you've been **really** helpful.
Thank you, Bunnies.

Now Baby has Bear **and** Book.
What a happy baby!

But, Bunnies,

WAIT!

Don't go!

Baby can't get to sleep without Blanket too.
Can you help one last time?

What's that, Bilal? Blanket has been

IN THE WASH?

OH NO!

Blanket's all squeaky clean!
It's hard and not-snuggly.
Blanket smells like . . .

NEW.

Baby will **never**
get to sleep now.

What are we going to do?

Betsy, you're a genius. That's a great idea!

We'll **hug** it,
and **tug** it . . .

Wheeee!

and then Blanket will be all

rumpled

and

crumpled

and smell of cuddles, just as Baby likes.

There you go, Baby. Blanket's all ready for bedtime.
Now Baby has Bear **and** Book **and** Blanket.

What a happy baby!

Wait a minute . . . Where's Bear?

BOBBIE!

Give Bear back to Baby, please.

Now Baby will go to sleep.

Night, night, Baby.

But what can be wrong?
We have Bear, Book and Blanket.
Nothing's missing.

IT'S THE PERFECT BEDTIME!

What's that, Barney?
Something **is** missing?
But . . . what?

Oh yes!

You're right! We missed . . .

. . . the **goodnight kiss.**
How could we forget?

Night, night, Baby.
Kiss, kiss.

It's time for bed
for you too, Bunnies. **SHHHHHHH.**

WHAT?

You want bears and books and blankets too?

Okay, well, here we go . . .

Night, night,

kiss, kiss . . .

EVERYONE.